To: Carol
From: Becky

PRESENTED TO

_____

FROM

_____

A Story of Christmas and All of Us

Roma Downey & Mark Burnett

FaithWords

New York | Boston | Nashville

www.bibleseries.tv

All Scriptures are taken from the *Holy Bible, New International Version*®. Copyright © 1973, 1979, 1984, Biblica. Used by permission of Zondervan. All rights reserved.

Photography by Joe Alblas and Casey Crawford

Editorial and design: Koechel Peterson & Associates, Inc., Minneapolis, Minnesota.

FaithWords
Hachette Book Group
237 Park Avenue
New York, NY 10017

www.faithwords.com

Printed in the United States of America

First Edition: October 2013

10 9 8 7 6 5 4 3 2

FaithWords is a division of Hachette Book Group, Inc.
The FaithWords name and logo are trademarks of Hachette Book Group, Inc.

The Hachette Speakers Bureau provides a wide range of authors for speaking events. To find out more, go to www.hachettespeakersbureau.com or call (866) 376-6591.

The publisher is not responsible for websites (or their content) that are not owned by the publisher.

LLCN: 2013944695

ISBN: 978-1-4555-7339-4

Let's honor Christmas

in our hearts

and try to keep it there all year long.

Five hundred years

have passed since the Jewish prophet Daniel's vision

of a great beast, dreadful and terrible and incredibly

strong, that would devour the entire world with its iron

teeth. Through long momentous years of war, conquest,

and subservience, this vision had become a reality as

the Romans had extended the mightiest empire in history

to include Palestine. Rome values the land of Israel for

its important military and trading routes between the

provinces of Syria to the north and Egypt in the south

and its tax revenues.

But Daniel had also had another vision in which he saw one like "the son of man," who would come to save the world and be given glory and authority and sovereign power. Peoples, nations, and every language group would worship him. He will be called the Prince of Peace, Holy of Holies, and the Lord God Almighty. Descended from the lineage of David, this man, like his forefather, will be called the King of the Jews, though he will rule over a very different kingdom, the kingdom of God.

The Jewish people have learned patience during their long

years under the boots of the Egyptians, Babylonians, Persians,

Greeks, and now Romans. At this time, they are ruled by a Roman

puppet named Herod the Great, the so-called King of the Jews,

who is only half Jewish and comes from a family that converted

to the faith. He has been married ten times, murdered

one wife, and will soon murder two of his sons.

He suffers from fits of paranoia, has been in

power for forty years, and owes his position

to none other than Julius Caesar.

The Jews live under Herod's oppression, which causes fear and tension, but they are allowed to practice their religion without fear of prosecution. So they pay the austere tax demanded by Rome, knowing the soldiers will go for now and leave them alone. They long for freedom in their land and for an end to poverty and wait in the hopes that the Messiah will come and rescue them from the senseless deaths at the hands of their oppressors. Little do they know that change is coming—and from the least likely of places.

THE REVOLUTION starts quietly and without notice in the small village of Nazareth surrounded by fields and olive groves in the province of Galilee. Joseph, a carpenter, sits in a small synagogue as an elder reads from the Torah, the Israelites' holy book. Joseph is a direct descendant of King David, and his life revolves around Scripture, work, and family. His time in the synagogue would normally be spent in quiet prayer and meditation, as is true of the men around him who have come to worship, lost in their communion with God.

But today, Joseph is lost—

in love.

A latticework screen separates the men and women. Joseph has purposely seated himself next to the divider, allowing him to sneak a look at his bride to be—Mary. She's the most beautiful girl he's ever seen.

"Mary, my betrothed," Joseph whispers to himself, making sure not to slip and begin mumbling the words loud enough for all to hear, causing a stir in the synagogue. "You have the most beautiful eyes I've ever seen. And the sweetest smile."

Mary, who is pure of heart, has been praying for an end to wickedness and sin and for the restoration of David's royal lineage. Her focus suddenly changes, and she catches Joseph staring at her. She blushes and turns away, but then glances back and meets Joseph's gaze. A sense of deep connection passes between them.

It is Mary who looks away first. Joseph forces himself to focus

on the words of the elder, but he finds it almost impossible. He

longs impatiently for the wondrous life that he and Mary will

build together once they are man and wife. Joseph is not a man

of great vision; but even if he were, he still could not possibly

imagine how extraordinary their lives will soon become. Every bit

of his faith in God will be required to understand what is about

to happen.

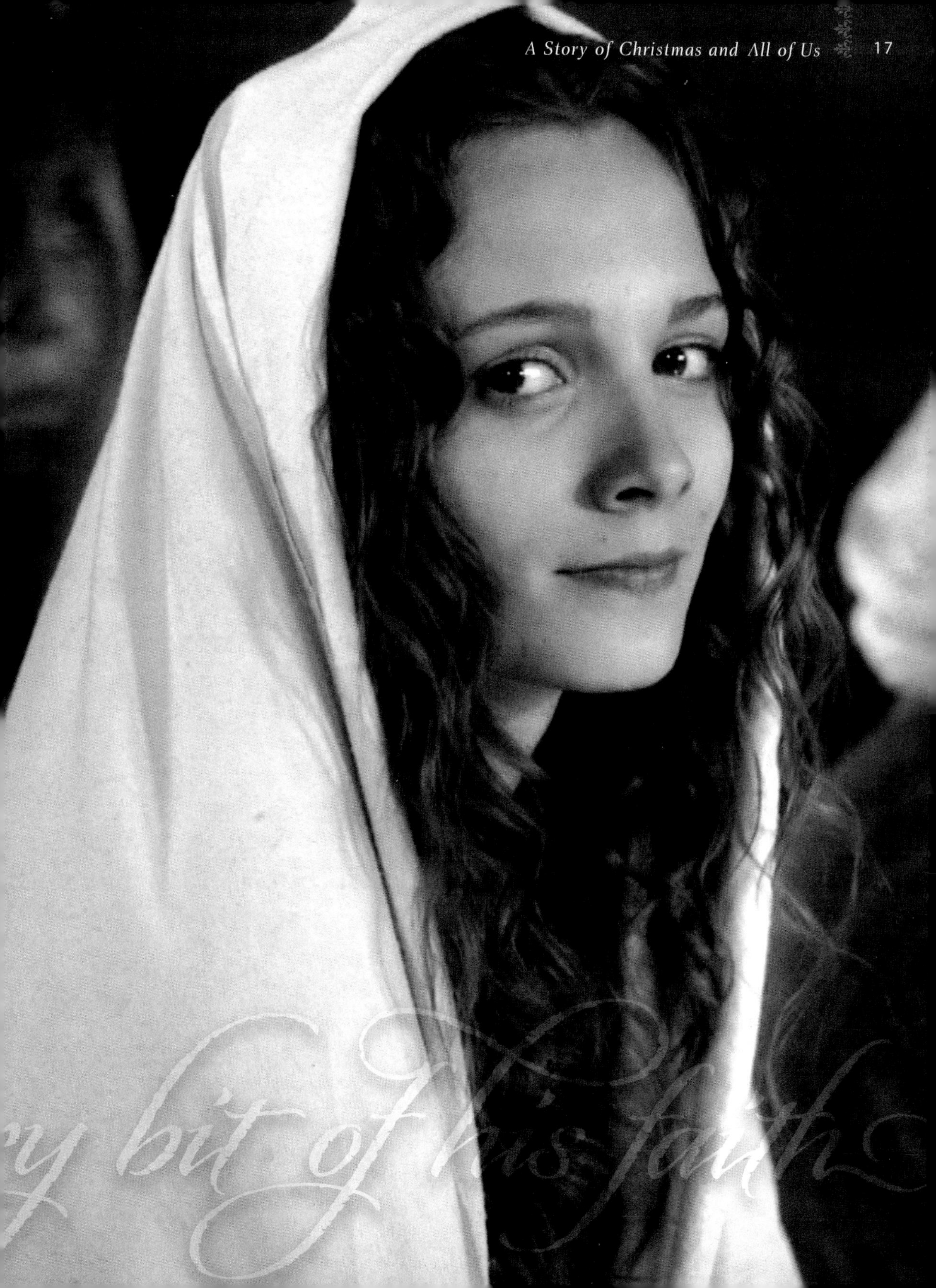
bit of his faith

OUTSIDE THE SYNAGOGUE, dust blows through the streets. The sound of marching feet is heard, then the clatter of metal. Swords, shields, and battle armor glint in the hot Judean sun as a body of Roman soldiers moves in lockstep up the empty lane accompanied by two well-dressed civilians—despised tax collectors. The enforcers have come to collect unpaid tribute to Rome.

The doors of the synagogue suddenly burst open, flooding the room with light. As the Roman officer enters and looks around the stunned congregation, the cantor stops his singing in mid flow. Nothing like this has ever happened before in their synagogue.

"In the name of Herod and Rome…

taxes are owed!"

Joseph is the first to react, jumping to his feet. "What is this?"

"We will take this man!" the Roman officer commands, pointing

to a poorly dressed farmer, whom two soldiers immediately

grab and drag out into the street.

"Can't you see you're interrupting the Scriptures?"

Joseph cries.

But the Roman officer ignores Joseph, having spotted the other man for whom they are searching, a frightened older man who is struggling to get to his feet, and the officer and another soldier move toward him.

Mary crosses the room to protect the old man, and the Roman officer is about to push her out of the way when Joseph steps in and blocks his way.

"This must be a mistake!" Joseph pleads. "We are worshiping God here."

This must be a mistake...

*Can't you see you're
interrupting the Scriptures?*

For a moment, the Roman pauses to regard Joseph's

challenge. But instead of getting angry, he cracks a cruel smile.

"Your god, your problem," he answers sarcastically, then thrusts

Joseph aside and grabs the man. "Come on, old man!"

Joseph's intervention has had the desired effect. The officer

has been distracted, and Mary is safe.

Out in the street, the Romans break into house after house,

emerging with bales of cloth, leather goods, sacks of fresh

fruit and grain, and even goats.

"Get back to your father's house," Joseph tells Mary as chaos has erupted in the streets. "Be quick!"

As Mary hurries toward home amid families and individuals being assaulted by the Romans, an angel of the Lord in a hooded cape stands on a walkway above the street keeping watch over her.

"Mary," Gabriel says softly, which she hears above the din of the street and causes her to stop and look for the mysterious voice's source. "Mary," he repeats, but she still sees no one. For a moment, she is frozen in place, shocked and fearful for her life.

Mary races on down the streets, while all that is around her seems to slip into slow motion. Coming to her father's house, she passes through the gate and slams it shut behind her, finally safe. As she turns into the courtyard, the angel approaches her from inside the dwelling.

"Don't be afraid, Mary," he speaks quietly, coming close to her. "The Lord is with you. You have found favor with God."

Mary takes a small involuntary step backward in shock as the angel slowly lowers his hood, then gasps for air as she tries to come to terms with what is happening.

"You will soon give birth to a son, and you are to call him Jesus. He will be great and will be known as the Son of the Most High."

"How can that be?" Mary asks in a half-trembling tone. "I am still a virgin."

"The Holy Spirit will come upon you," the angel continues.

"And the power of the Most High will overshadow you. Don't be

afraid." Mary's hands press against her midsection as if she can

already feel an energy there.

Mary gasps and slowly reaches out her hands and takes

his, then says, "I am the Lord's servant. May it be to me as you

have said."

"The holy one to be born will be called the Son of God,"

he whispers.

Then, as suddenly as he had appeared, the angel is gone. Mary runs her fingertips over her abdomen. "Jesus," she whispers. "I am to name him Jesus."

But the angel never said being God's servant would be easy.

Mary hides her pregnancy for as long as she can, not knowing how

she can explain it to Joseph. For the first few months she moves

away to live in the hill country with her cousin Elizabeth, who is

also pregnant and will become the mother of John the Baptist.

When she returns, it is obvious that she is with child, and

Joseph notices immediately when he sees her in the street. "Mary!"

he cries out, pursuing her, but she does not stop. He pushes past

a woman and calls out again, "Mary!" Finally catching her by the

shoulder, he demands, "Tell me what's going on, Mary. Please!"

"Not here," she insists with tears in her eyes.

"Then where?"

It is forbidden for the two of them to be alone together until marriage, but she has no choice. She leads Joseph to her father's sheep shed and closes the door behind them. She removes her robe ever so slightly, revealing her pregnant stomach to Joseph, confirming what he has suspected. His eyes squeeze shut.

"Mary? Who did this to you? What have you done?" He is angry, feeling betrayed, confused, and then a fool. By the law, she is guilty of adultery. "What on earth have you done?"

"Joseph, let me explain." Mary struggles to control herself. She's never seen Joseph like this. Normally he's quiet and strong; now he's on the verge of tears. She grabs hold of his calloused hands. She is so desperately in love with this man that it hurts to see his heart so broken. She forces him to look in her eyes. Their future hangs on the words she is about to say—along with the fate of all mankind. "Joseph," she whispers. "There has been no one. I swear to you. I am a virgin."

"Well, there's been someone," Joseph blurts out, stepping away from her in disgust. "I'm not stupid!"

"This is God's work," Mary says gently. "I don't know why I would be chosen, but I'm telling you the truth. An angel of the Lord appeared to me, telling me that I would be with child. He is to be the Messiah. You must believe me."

He looks at her in disbelief. "I thought I knew you. . . ."

She reaches for his hands and pleads, "Please, Joseph. I need you to be the father of this child—the child of God. Please, my love. Please trust me!"

"I want to believe," he says softly, gazing into her eyes. "But God would not send the Messiah to people like us."

Then he drops her hands, walks away, and doesn't look back.

Only then does this mountain of a man let himself cry.

JOSEPH HAS A HOUSE to build out on the edge of town, but it can wait. He wanders the streets of Nazareth alone and in a daze, mumbling to himself. "What do we say? What do we tell our parents? Of course, I must disown her. There's no other choice." But the grief that comes with the mere thought of a life without Mary soon sits on his chest like the weight of an elephant, taking his breath away. The hard truth is that if he leaves Mary, both she and the child will become outcasts. They will live on the street, begging for handouts and fending for themselves. "God help me," Joseph prays. "Help me find a way to do the right thing."

Joseph leans against a wall, lost in his thoughts. People stare at him, but he doesn't care. Joseph's head droops and his shoulders sag, then he closes his eyes and prays, "If this is your work, Lord, please help. Help us. . . ."

Help me find a way

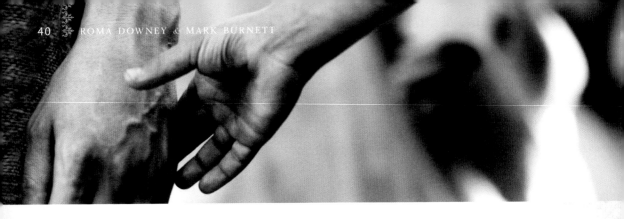

Just then a young child on the street reaches out, takes Joseph's hand, and he falls into a dream state.

"Joseph," a voice says. "Joseph, son of David." The angel Gabriel now stands powerfully before Joseph, the hood of his cloak pulled down, exposing his soft and tender face. His eyes seem to peer straight into Joseph's soul. Gabriel reaches for Joseph's hands. "Be at peace. Take Mary as your wife," he commands. "She is telling you the truth. She is pure. The child that she carries is from God."

A stunned Joseph stares into the divine beauty of the angel. The weight upon his heart is gone. He wipes a tear of joy from his eye, and in that instant Gabriel is gone. Joseph emerges from his dream elated and races to Mary's home to tell her that he believes her. Their baby will be named Jesus.

One translation of the name is "God rescues." It also means "God saves." To many in Israel, the notion of a Messiah is a conquering king like David, a savior who will deliver them from Roman oppression. God, however, has something far bigger in mind. God will remain God, yet also become human in Jesus. He will save not just Israel but the entire world.

PERIODICALLY THE ROMANS demand a national census. No matter where they are residing, all the male citizens must return to the town of their family lineage and be counted for taxation and bureaucratic control. Now happily married, Joseph and Mary strap their belongings to the back of a donkey and set off from Nazareth for the town of Bethlehem, the city where King David was born. The morning air is cold as Joseph lifts Mary onto the donkey, where she will ride. She is far too pregnant to walk the eighty-mile journey.

Normally, it is a four-day trek to Bethlehem, but the threat of bandits on the highway has Joseph planning on taking a slower, safer, and circuitous route that will add an extra three days. He leans in to kiss her belly, grabs the reins, and leads them out onto the dusty road at the edge of town, with the baby due any day.

They soon clear a low rise leading away from Nazareth, and the early morning sky opens wide before them. Mary and Joseph are alone against the world. They know this is the way it is going to be for them.

But others are being drawn toward them. . . .

Just

outside faraway Babylon,

a sage and astrologer named Balthazar gazes out at the amazing

heavenly light hovering over Jerusalem. He is wealthy beyond

measure, dressed in fine silk clothing. Soldiers surround him

on this hillside, there to protect him against bandits on his long

journey. Balthazar has followed the star all the way from Persia,

riding his camel up and over the mountains into Babylon.

They ride by night and sleep by day so that they may more

easily follow the star.

Balthazar is a learned man who has studied the prophecies of many faiths, and he believes the star to be a sign from God. His escorts are quickly bored by the unusual sight, which they consider a mere cosmic fluke. Balthazar studies it at length every night, certain that two great forces are coming together before his eyes: first, God's command of the heavens; second, and equally powerful, the words of God's prophets that are known beyond Israel's borders.

"A star shall come out of Jacob," Balthazar recites the ancient prophecy of Moses in the Book of Numbers. "And a scepter shall rise out of Israel." Balthazar is certain this star portends the arrival of a great leader. He feels blessed to be alive for such a momentous occasion. "Perhaps it is true. Perhaps the prophets of Israel were right," he says in awe. He hurriedly rallies his men, climbs back on his camel, and sets off into the night. He is bound for Jerusalem, eager to deliver the Good News.

But Balthazar is taking the Good News to the one man in Israel

who doesn't want to hear it: King Herod. The man who rules Israel

for the Romans, dominating his fellow Jews under his iron will,

clings to power with a paranoid desperation. Even the slightest

rumors about an attempt to take away his throne are dealt with

immediately. All dissent is crushed. All dissenters are killed.

Now he waddles through his palace, down a marble-and-gilt

corridor lined with rich tapestries. Herod wears velvet slippers,

his feet splayed and shuffling. Each step causes him extreme pain.

His breathing is labored, and his bald head is shiny with sweat.

Herod's captain of the guard follows close behind, careful not to step alongside the slow-moving king, for that would be seen as an attempt at equality, which would enflame Herod and may result in this career soldier losing his cushy, powerful position.

"You bring me news?" asks Herod, gasping for breath between each word.

"More trouble from the God-fearing fanatics, I'm afraid," replies the captain.

"Fine," Herod says, issuing a death warrant. "If they love God so much, send them to be with him."

MARY AND JOSEPH are well aware of Herod's evil—and that their journey to Bethlehem will bring them within just five miles of the royal palace. It is dusk now. Joseph makes camp on a barren hillside, even though there's enough daylight to travel a few more miles.

"I could go on," Mary insists, her face lined in weariness and the discomfort of yet another long day riding the donkey.

Joseph smiles and adds another piece of kindling to the fire he's building. "You need to rest. I'm tired and so is the donkey. Let's stop here."

A boy steps forth, carrying a bundle of kindling. Without saying a word, he hands it to Joseph, who accepts it and sees the boy's father tending a flock of sheep in the distance. Joseph nods to the shepherd in thanks, even as the boy scurries away.

Their journey has been filled with a dozen such

kindnesses. Mary and Joseph are both coming to grips

with her imminent motherhood of the Messiah.

From now on, all generations will call her blessed.

Mary curls up by the fire as a hard gust of wind rakes the hillside. Joseph sits down at her side and covers her with a rough blanket. She falls asleep, even as the great star once again rises into night. Joseph will stay up most of the night, making sure the fire stays strong and keeps his beloved and her unborn child warm.

HEROD GAZES OUT into the coming night, lying on his couch and eating his dinner. He sees the unusual star shining in the east, but thinks nothing of it until the lavishly dressed Balthazar is escorted into the royal chamber and announced. Balthazar gives a small bow, as from king to king. Herod manages a tiny nod of the head in response.

"Balthazar. Welcome," Herod mumbles, having struggled to sit up and taking his wine goblet in hand. "Wine?"

"You are very gracious, Majesty," Balthazar replies. "But I'd rather not."

"So what brings you here, O prince?" Herod demands, his
voice echoing off the marble pillars.

"I just want to know if there is an official word about these
signs?" Balthazar asks, trying to be as deferential as possible. He
knows Herod's reputation for whimsical evil.

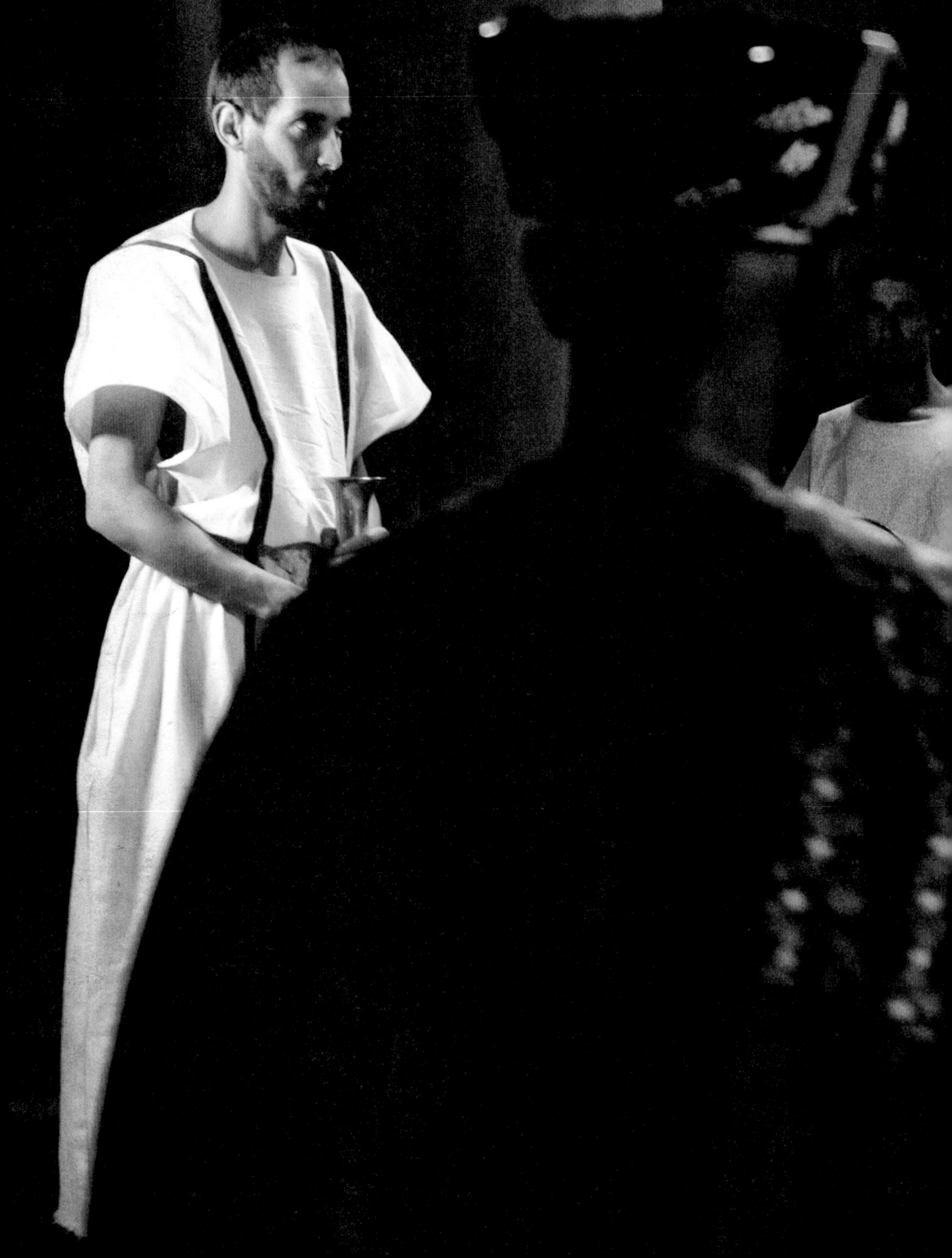

Herod stares at his guest, deciding how best to deal with him. "What signs?" he asks.

"The star. The new star rises in the east. I have followed its progress. The star is a sign that a great man is coming."

Herod glares at him. Not wanting to ignite Herod's legendary temper, Balthazar quickly motions for his men to lay out their elaborate charts of the stars on the marble floor. He then goes on to explain how he was guided by the star to Jerusalem.

But Herod isn't listening. He stares intently at Balthazar, then finally says, "Every week someone claims to be the chosen one. But those are mostly madmen in the marketplace—easily ignored and just as easily silenced. So are you telling me that I should take your charts and your belief in a chosen one seriously?"

"Very seriously, sire." Balthazar once again motions for his

men to step forward. This time they hold gifts in their arms.

"We bring this chosen one presents fit for a king."

That gets Herod's attention. "King?"

"Yes, Majesty. This man will become King of the Jews."

An awkward silence fills the chamber, making it quiet

enough to hear a snake slither. Balthazar realizes he has just

said something wrong.

Herod's eyebrows rise. "Really?" he says through pursed lips.

"Yes, Majesty. This is prophesied from God. The heavens

testify to his arrival."

Herod smiles warmly, feigning a religiosity that he does not possess. "It has been testified? Really? If that is so, then we must do something immediately to pay homage."

Herod summons the captain of the guard and whispers in his ear. "Bring me the priests and scribes. I need a word with them." Then Herod dismisses Balthazar with a wave of his hand, walks to a terrace and gazes out over Jerusalem. There, in the midst of darkness and turmoil, rises the star, which he curses. "I am king of the Jews. And I will forever remain king of the Jews," he vows to himself. "I will keep my throne."

AS JOSEPH AND MARY make their approach down the rocky hillside on the outskirts of Bethlehem in the dark of night, the rain begins to fall, first lightly, then it begins to pour.

"Hold on!" Joseph calls out, picking up the pace as he leads the donkey by its rope.

Mary groans. "It won't be long now, Joseph," she says.

"We're almost there, Mary. I'll hurry!" he replies, bracing himself against the cold rain and wondering where they will find shelter for the night. He knows that thousands of other travelers have made their way to Bethlehem for the census and overwhelmed the limited places for lodging. Joseph pulls the donkey under a stone archway, at least out of the rain and wind and steps back to Mary, who is soaked and desperate.

Hold on!

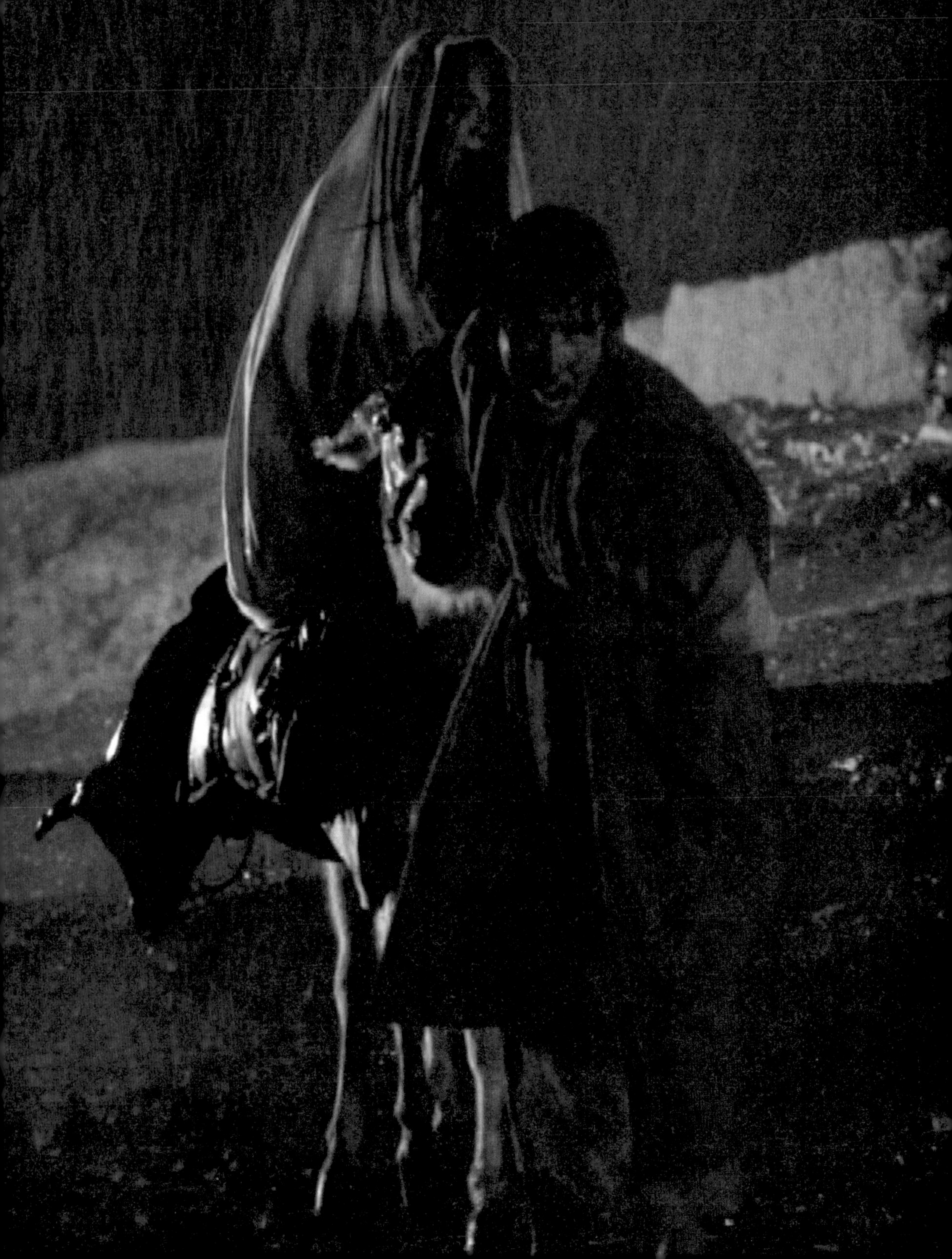

Mary's stiff cold fingers spasm as they lock around his arm,

and she cries out in pain. "Joseph! The baby is coming!"

"I'll find a place!" Joseph explains, then leaves Mary and the

donkey and runs into the city, searching for some place warm

and private where she can deliver the baby. But no such shelter

is found in Bethlehem this night. Joseph is turned away time

and time again. The innkeepers are kind but insistent: there

is no room in Bethlehem for Mary and Joseph.

The shepherds stand watch over their flocks outside Bethlehem, waiting for the moment when the rain clouds will part and reveal the brilliant star they have become used to seeing each night.

And there it is.

The sheep calm down as the night settles into a time of quiet. And the shepherds, shivering from the damp of night, sit back and stare at the star, wondering what it means.

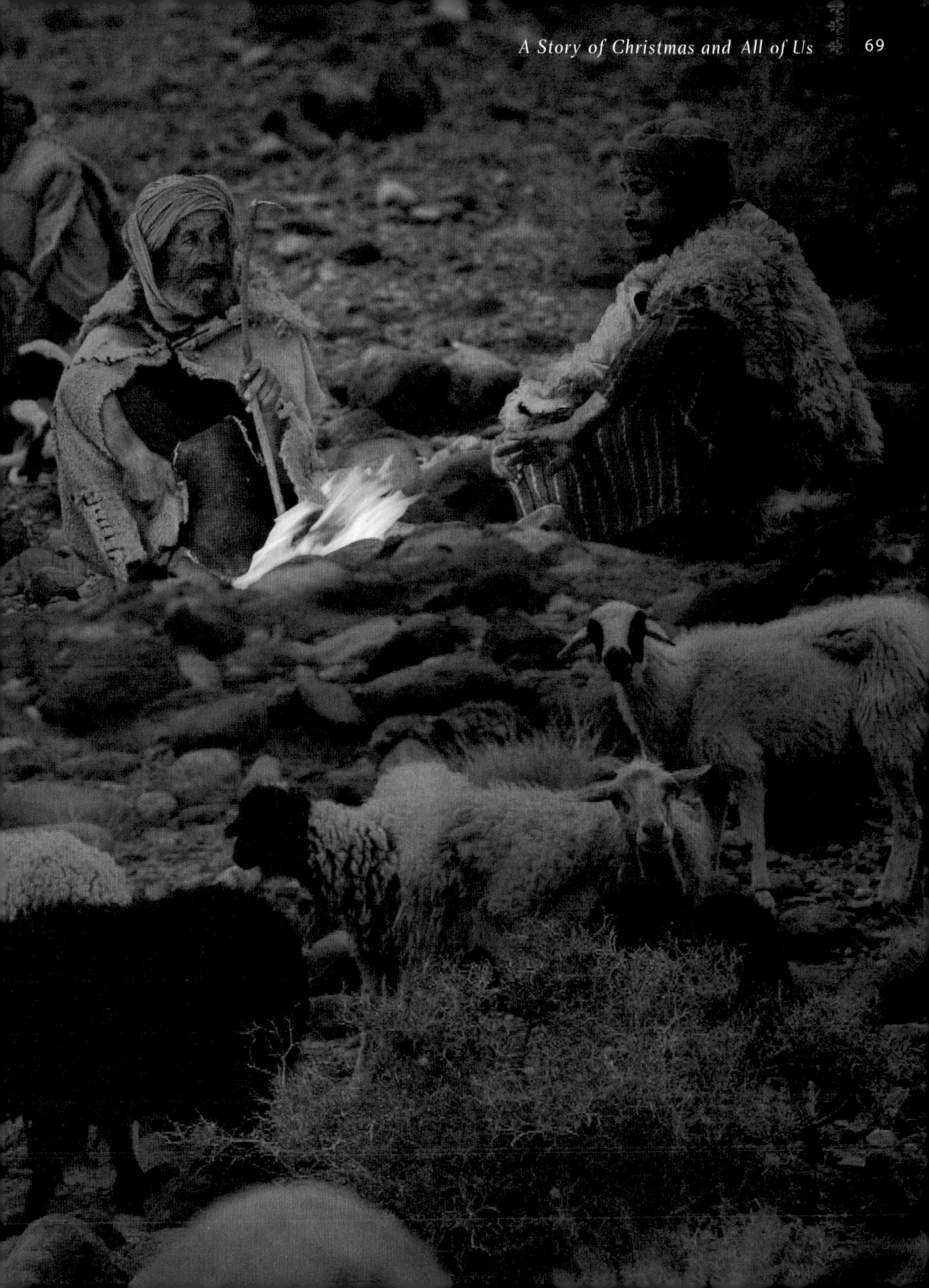

HEROD IS ALSO STUDYING the star, though not with the same sense of tranquility as the shepherds. Thanks to Balthazar's alert, he has demanded to see all that has been written about the prophesied "King of the Jews." A half-dozen priests and scribes furiously tear through pages of sacred texts in the temple library as Herod paces. His blotched and bloated face is red with fury. "Find it!" he screams again and again. "Find the traitorous prophecy!"

The scribes anxiously drag piles of scrolls from the shelves. Sweat pours from their faces in the fetid heat and dust.

"Here!" one priest yells with excitement. "In Micah."

"Read it," demands Herod.

"'He shall feed his flock in the strength of God, and they shall live secure.'"

"Is that all?" asks a puzzled Herod.

Another priest has found a different reference in Scripture.

"No, lord, there's more. This is from Isaiah: 'Therefore the Lord himself will give a sign . . . the virgin will conceive and give birth to a son, and will call him Immanuel.'"

"It is written…"

An elderly priest, suddenly unafraid of speaking up, adds
another sentence: "'And he will be called Wonderful Counselor,
Mighty God, Everlasting Father, Prince of Peace.'"

The priest finishes and looks over to see Herod staring at
him intently. "I'm the one who brings peace," the king snarls.
"Do you think some child can do that?"

Silence.

Then the elderly priest clears his throat. "It is written,"
he says solemnly.

Herod charges at the man, grabbing him by the robe. "Is it? Is it now? Well, then, is it written where this mighty prince, this answer to all prayer and problems, will be born?"

The elderly priest is unruffled. "In Bethlehem. It will be Bethlehem. Micah says, 'You Bethlehem . . . out of you will come a ruler who will shepherd my people, Israel—'"

The captain of the guard comes to drag the elderly priest away. But the old man will not be silenced, and even as he is pulled from the temple library, soon to meet his fate, he keeps reciting prophecy. "'Israel will be abandoned until the time when she who is in labor gives birth. And the rest of his brothers return to join the Israelites. He will stand and shepherd his flock in the strength of the Lord.

"'And his greatness

will reach

to the ends

of the earth.'"

MARY HAS GONE INTO LABOR, but Joseph still hasn't found a place for her to give birth. He races back to her, taking the donkey by the rope and leading them into the city. All that matters to Mary is safely bringing her child into the world.

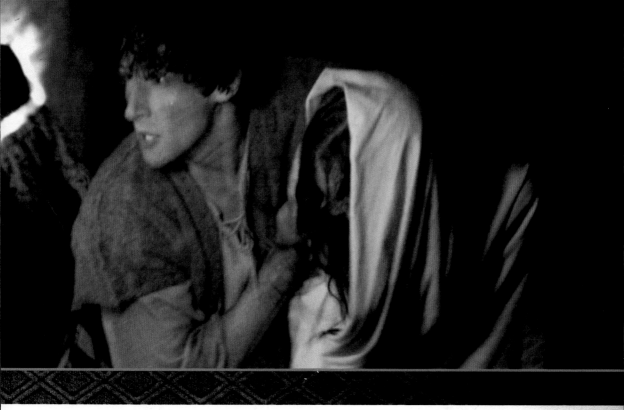

"Help us!" Joseph screams out above the noise of the storm.

Suddenly, Mary slides off the donkey and begins to collapse

to the ground. Joseph runs to her and holds her up as a local

innkeeper runs out of his house with a torch.

"Help us, please," Joseph pleads to him as Mary sobs.

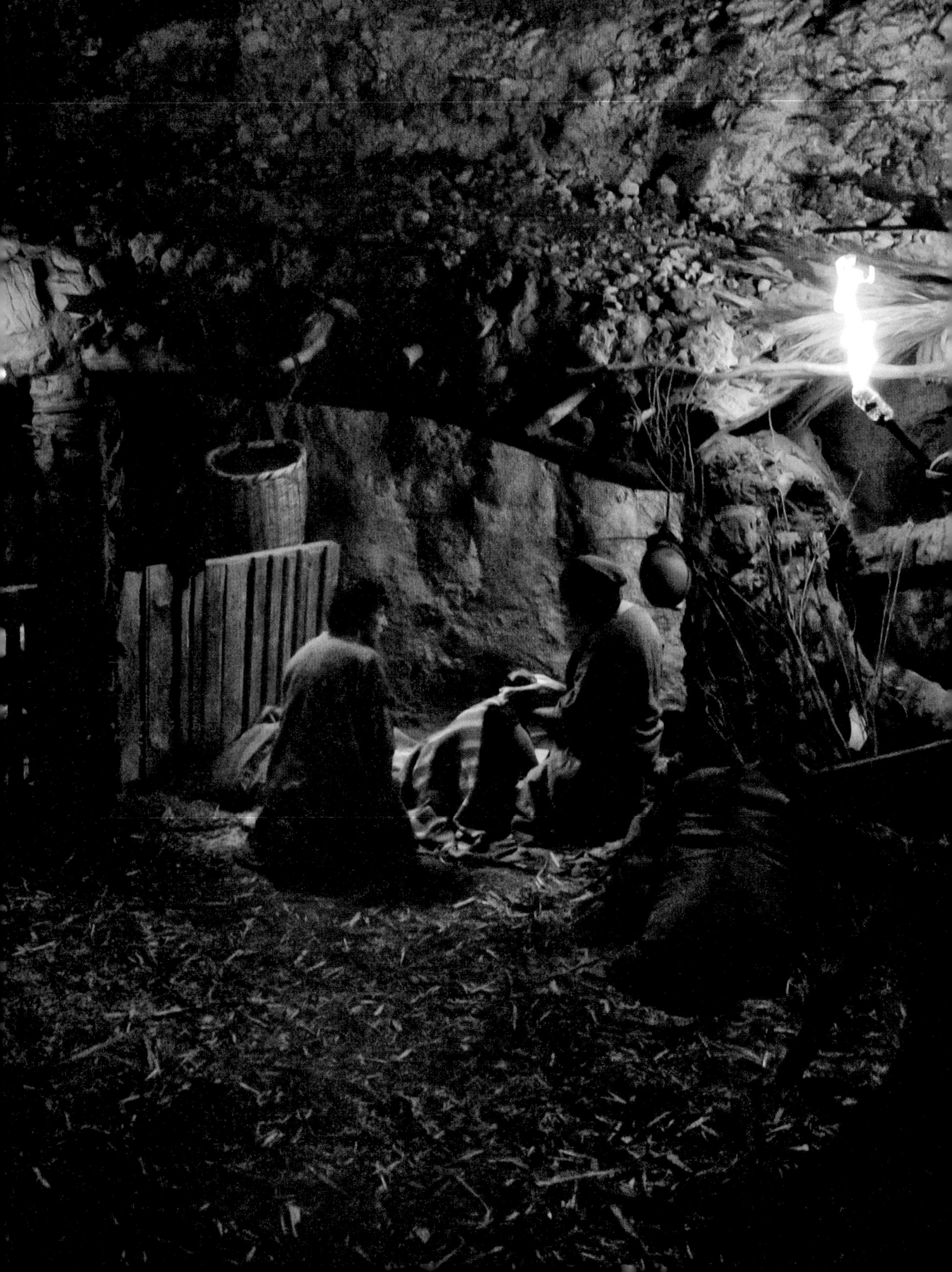

The innkeeper takes the donkey as the huddled figure of his wife emerges from the house and takes pity upon them, directing them toward a small cave used as a barn—called a grotto—smelling of animal waste and grain. Sheep and cows clutter the small space. Joseph and Mary eagerly follow the kind woman inside the sanctuary, where it is at least dry and warm.

The others clear a space, and Mary sinks down in the straw. It's only a few more minutes before the village midwife arrives, and just in time.

This baby is coming.

HEROD HAS RETURNED to his palace from the temple library. The words of the priests ring in his ears as he makes his way across his courtyard. As if the visit from Balthazar had begun a long series of very bad news, Herod is shocked to see another entourage enter his palace to offer their regards. Two Nubian potentates, dressed in elaborate robes and headgear, point to the star in wonder.

"More of them," Herod mutters to himself. "More of them! What's going on? Is the whole world in on this? These people come here to my country, to my palace, and ask me about the king who is coming to take my place."

But Herod's mind is devious, and by the time he reaches the Magi, his tone and expression have changed. "Gentlemen," he says sweetly, "you are most welcome. I have the most amazing news for you: the boy king that you are looking for will be born in the town of Bethlehem." He smiles broadly. "When you find him, please come and tell me precisely where he can be found so that I can go pay homage. More than anyone, it is my solemn duty to do so." Suddenly the king coughs hard, and blood leaks from the corner of his mouth and his face grows pale. It is quite clear that Herod is seriously ill. His body is ravaged by infection.

"But should you be traveling in your condition?" asks one of the Magi.

"Yes," Herod says solemnly, wiping his mouth with the back of his hand. "Even in my condition."

IN THE SOFT GLOW of the torch-lit cave, the midwife gently wraps the tiny newborn in swaddling clothing and hands him to Joseph, who holds the baby up to the light. A smile of wonder crosses his face, for he has never known such joy. She brings the child to Mary. "Thanks be to God," he says.

Mary tenderly holds her son. She is so taken with the child that she can't stop staring at him. Mary has never seen anything so precious nor anything that fills her heart with such love than her baby, and her light sobs are turned to soft laughter of wonderment. Her face transforms from tired and drained to radiant joy, and Joseph is overwhelmed.

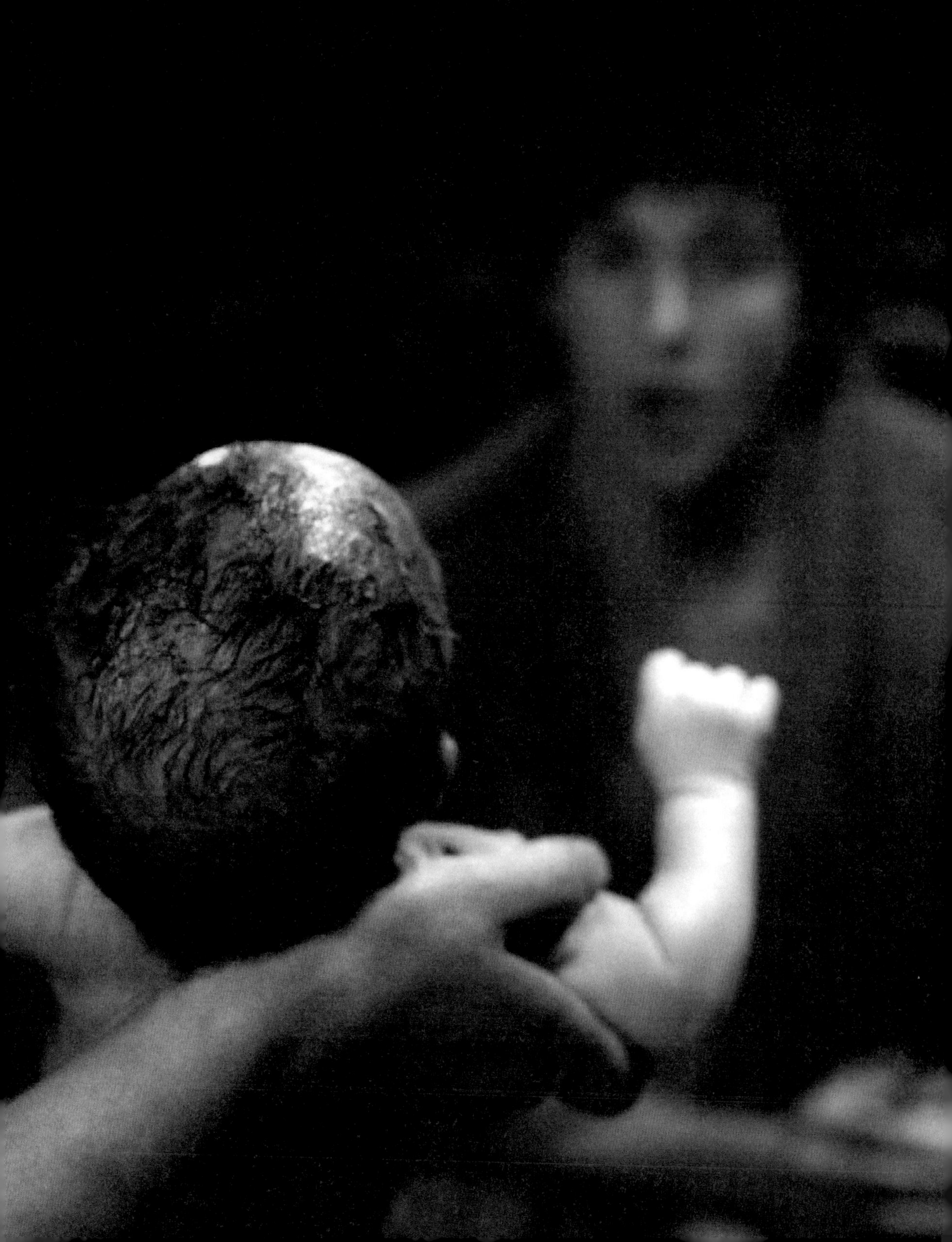

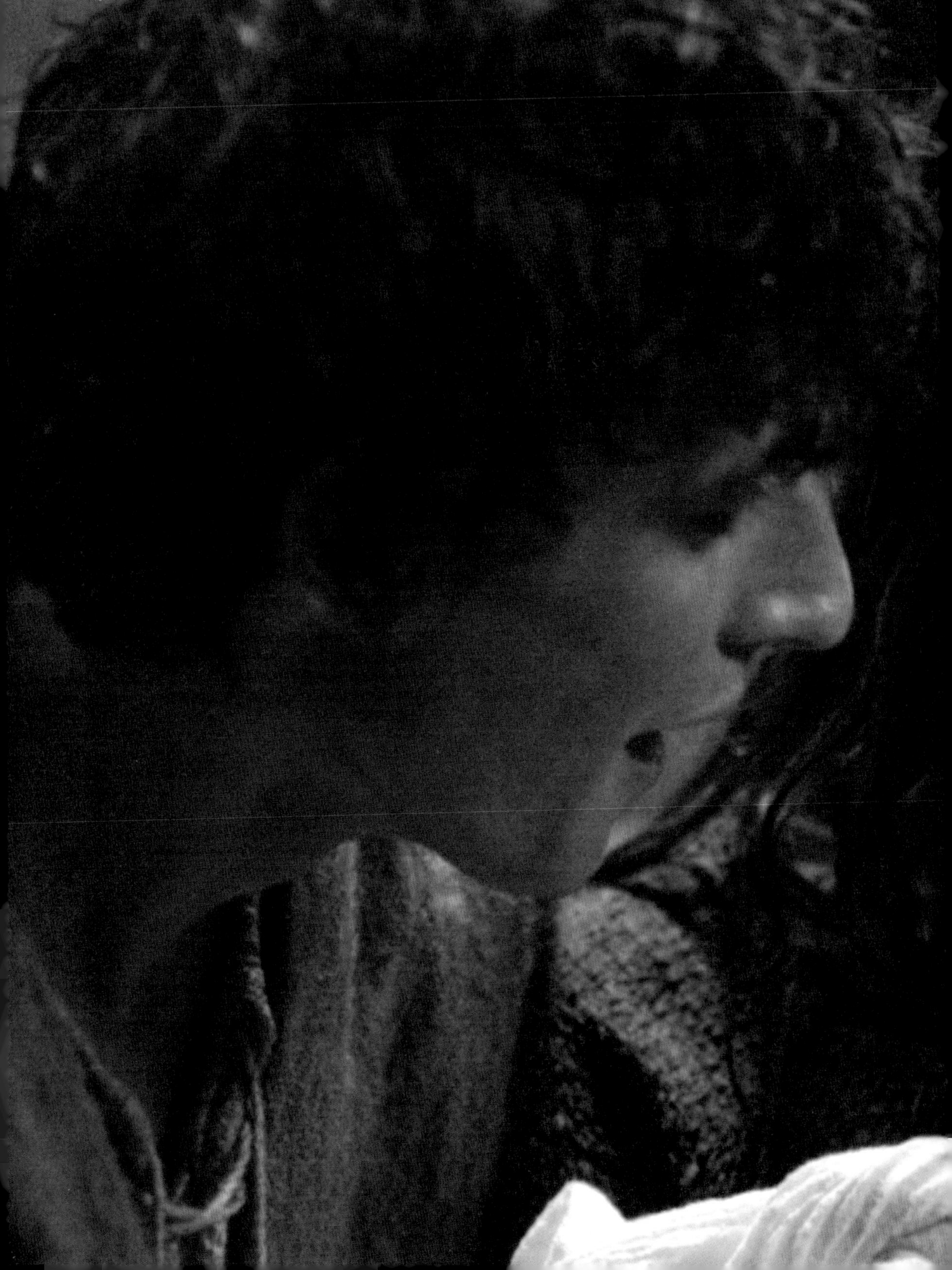

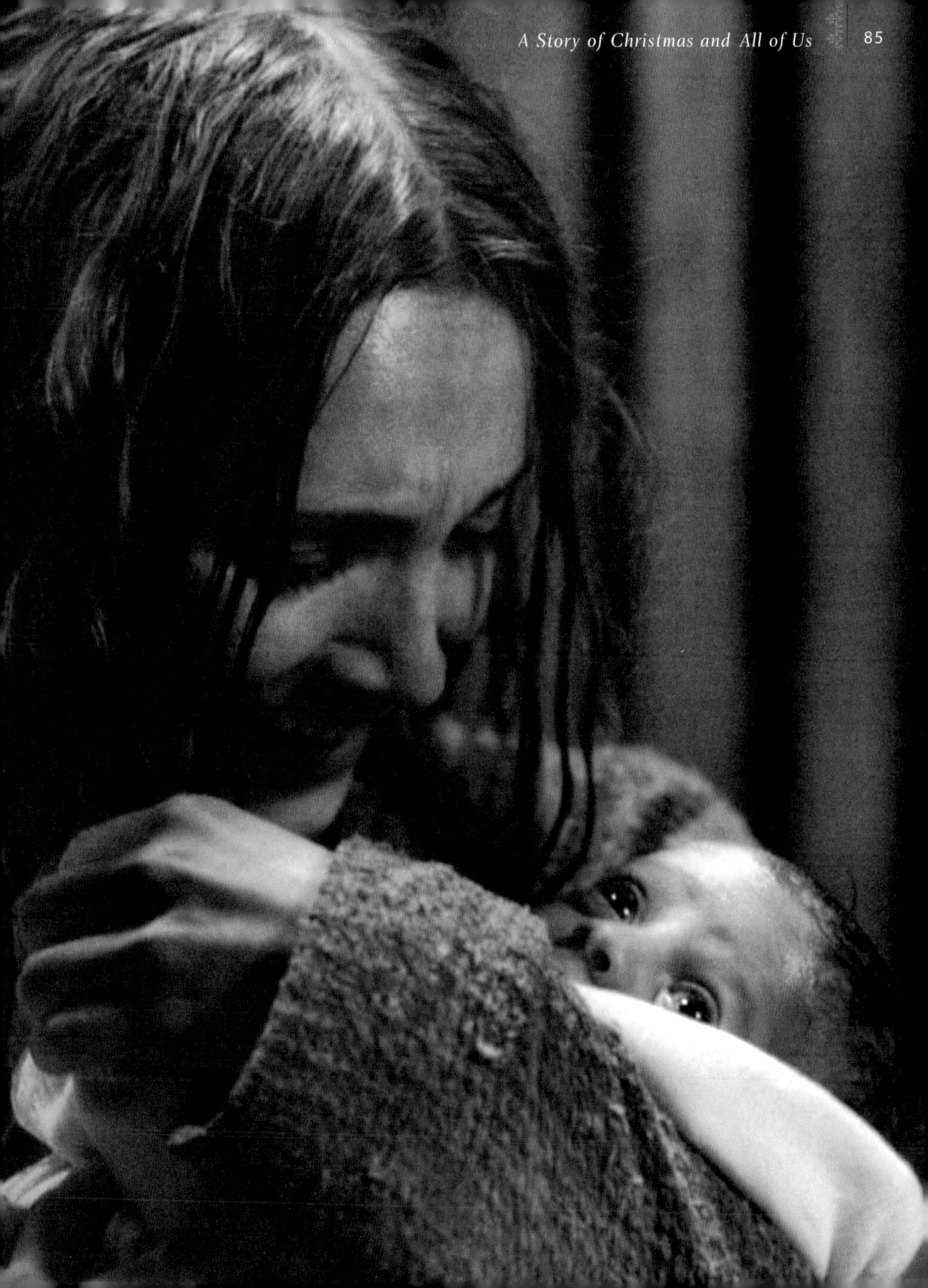

As far as Mary and Joseph know, only they are aware that this child is special. But when Joseph looks up, a crowd starts to gather in the cramped barn. The star has led many to this site. The same angelic intervention that brought Mary and Joseph to Bethlehem has also spread the news to those who need to hear it most: locals, shepherds, neighbors, and ordinary people. These are the ones whom Jesus has come to save, and for them to be standing in this small barn on this cold night is a moment unlike aany other in history. They are witnessing the dawning of a new era— the fulfillment of the new covenant between God and humanity.

Having left Herod's palace behind and nearing Bethlehem,

the Nubian wise men greet and fall into step with Prince Balthazar,

who is atop an adorned camel. They ride elegantly on their camels,

ecstatic about the prospect of meeting this great new savior. None

of them completely realizes who Jesus is and what he represents,

but on this night, in their hearts, Bethlehem feels like it is the

center of the universe.

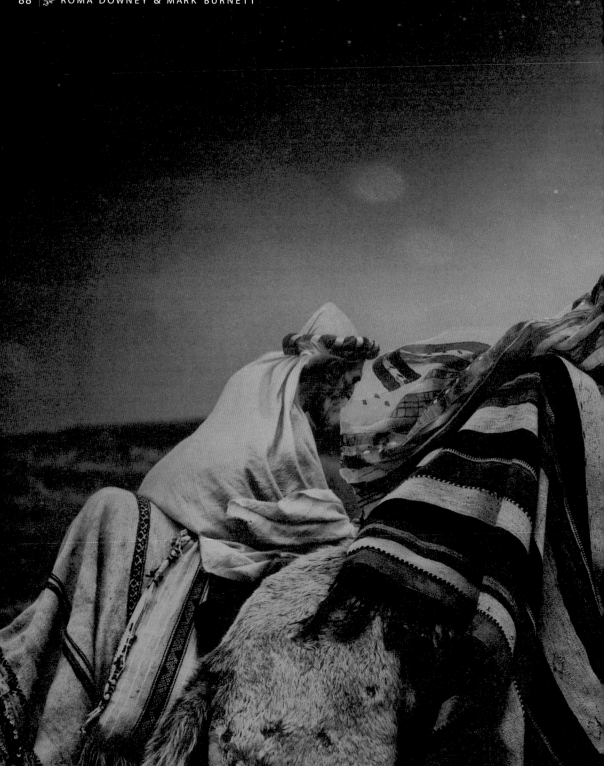

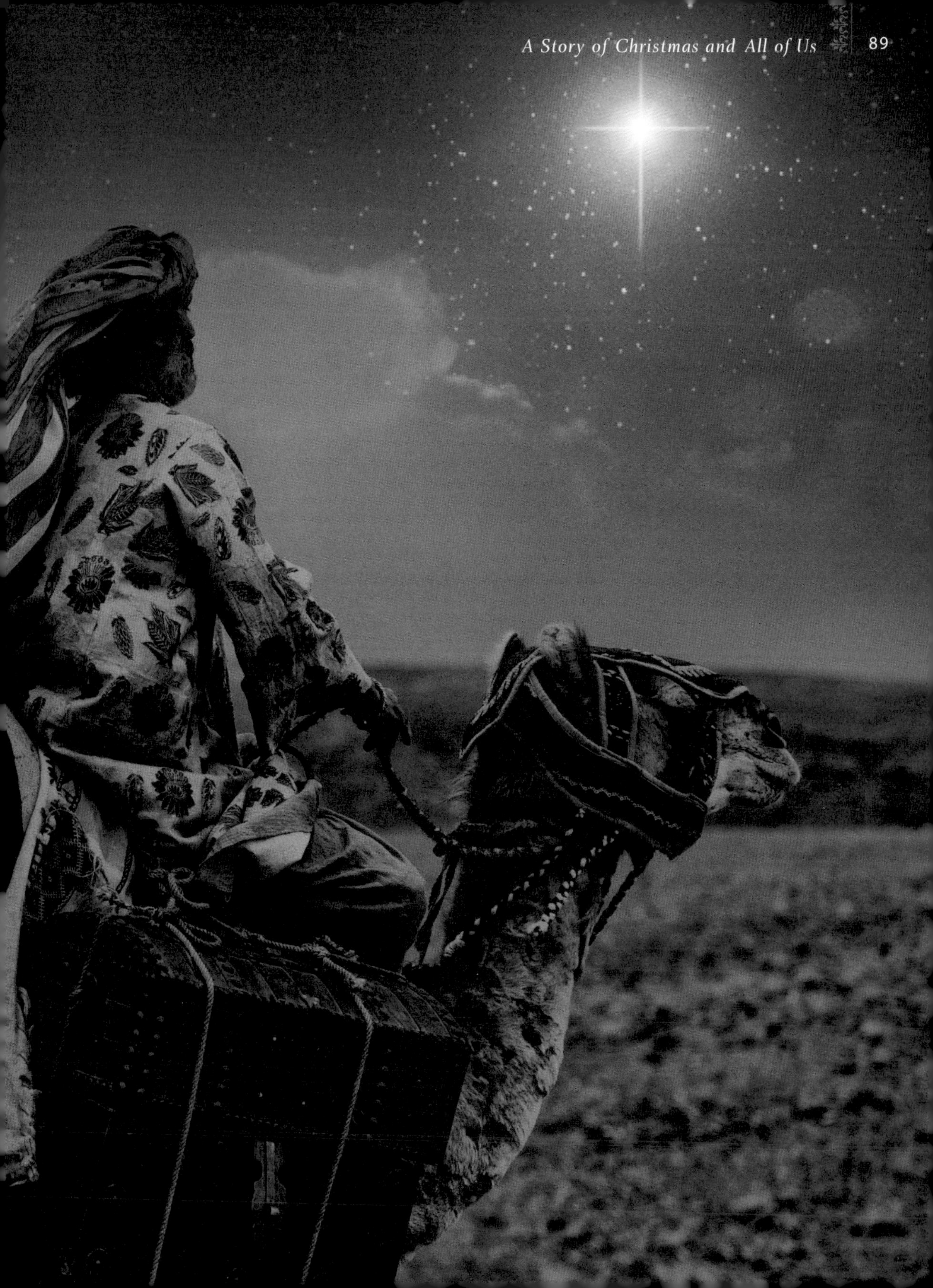

In the grotto, the crowd offers

prayers and small gifts to the child.

Some bow, while others weep with joy.

A young shepherd steps forward to

offer something far more precious:

a lamb without blemish.

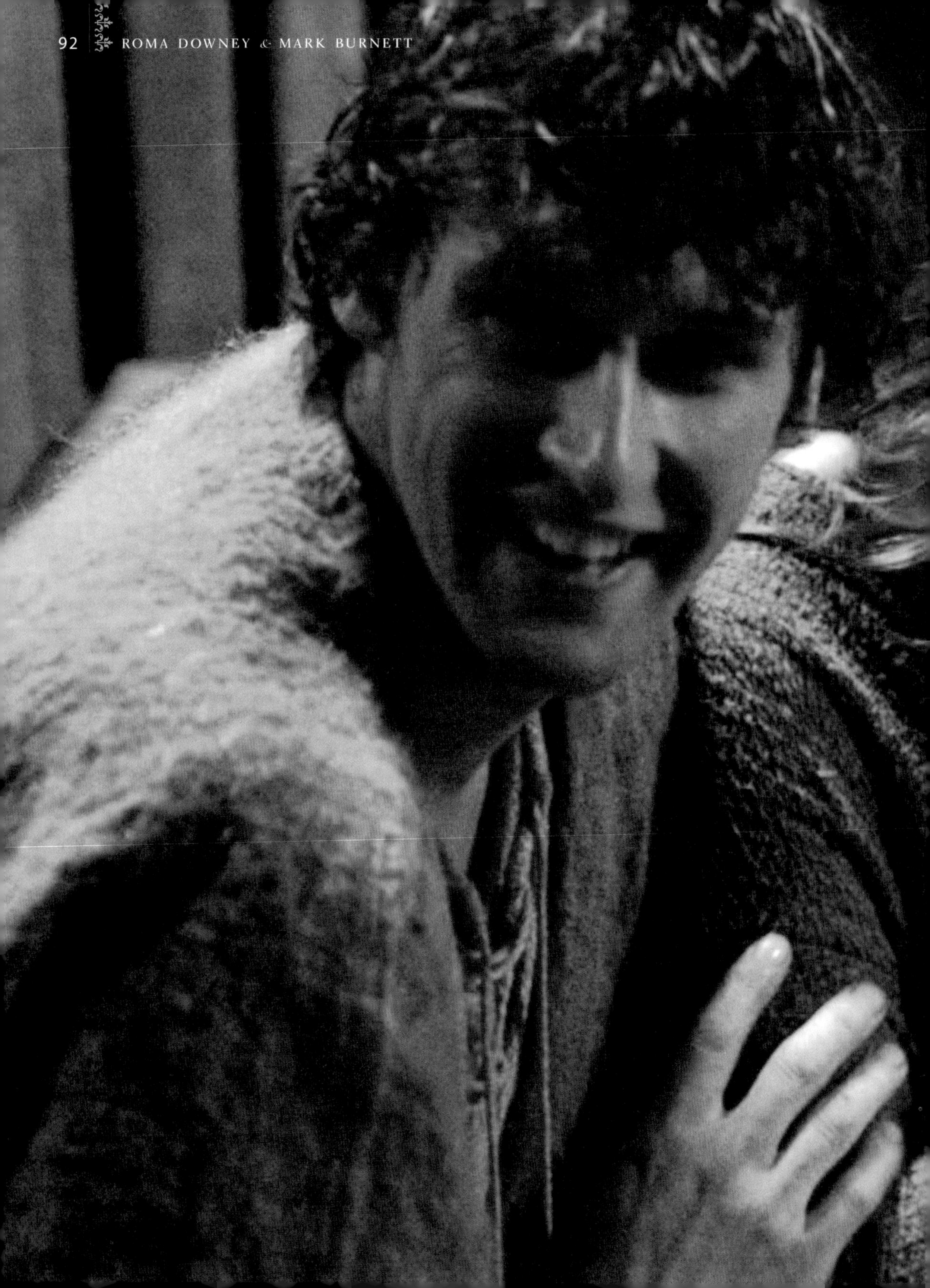

Joseph is thankful, but the truth is that he doesn't fully appreciate the gift. He smiles at Mary. Then a reflection near the grotto door catches Joseph's attention. His smile fades. The mass of farm workers, children, and shepherds part as royal attendants quietly and very efficiently clear a path. The crowd backs away, their eyes lowered in deference.

Joseph is uneasy. The last thing he wants is trouble.

your son is

the chosen king

Balthazar steps forward followed by the two Magi. He has changed into his finest robes, and the light catches the glint of gold in his headdress. His behavior is not regal, however. "I am humbled," he murmurs, as he drops to his knees along with the two Nubian princes and presents their precious gifts for the newborn child. Balthazar looks to Mary and says to her, "Lady, I believe your son is the chosen king of his people." Joseph realizes that he should bow to Balthazar, but before he can, Balthazar asks Mary, "What is his name?"

Mary gently kisses her
child on the forehead.
"Jesus," she tells Balthazar,
surprised to see that
the Nubians have come
to see their child.
"His name is Jesus."

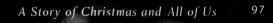

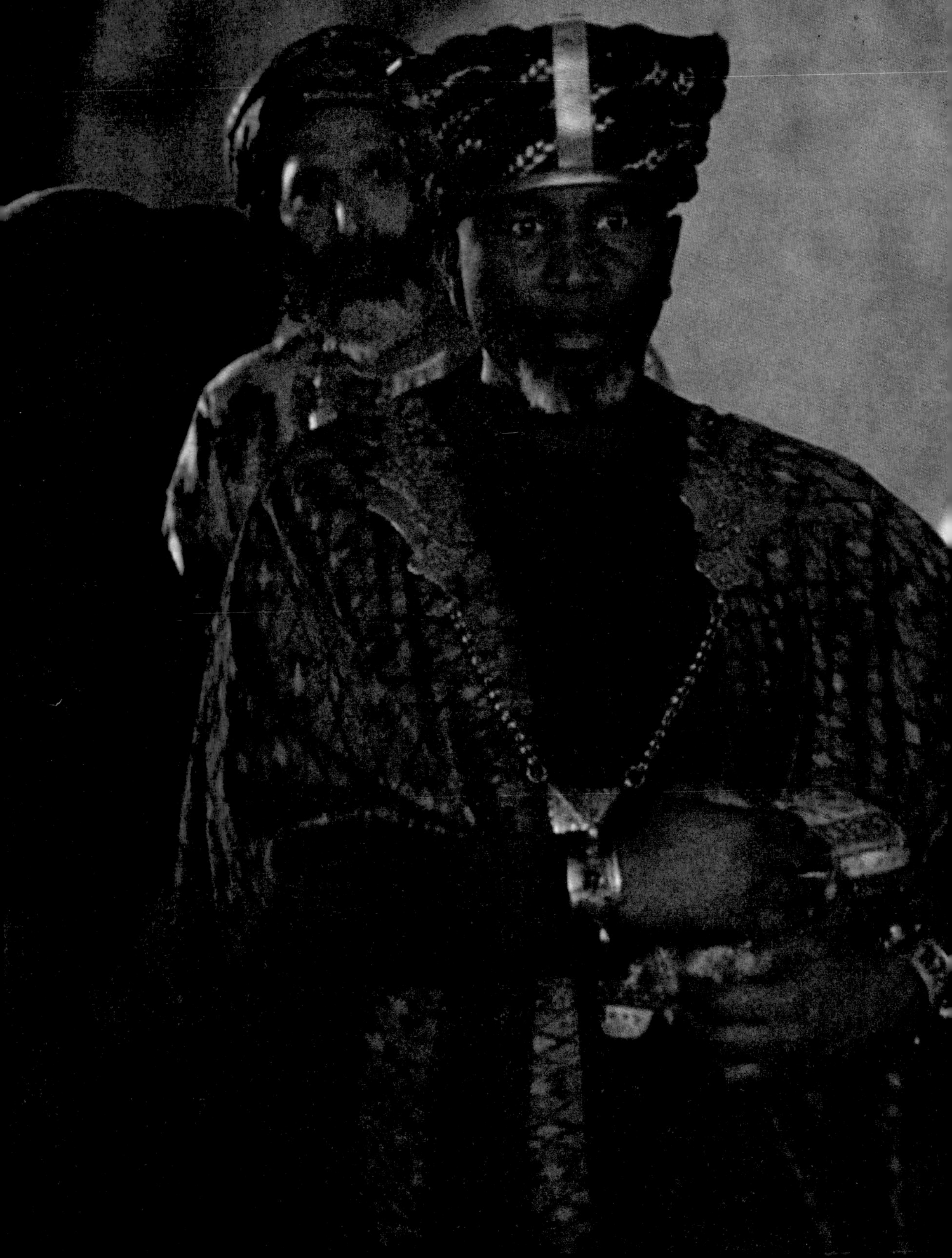

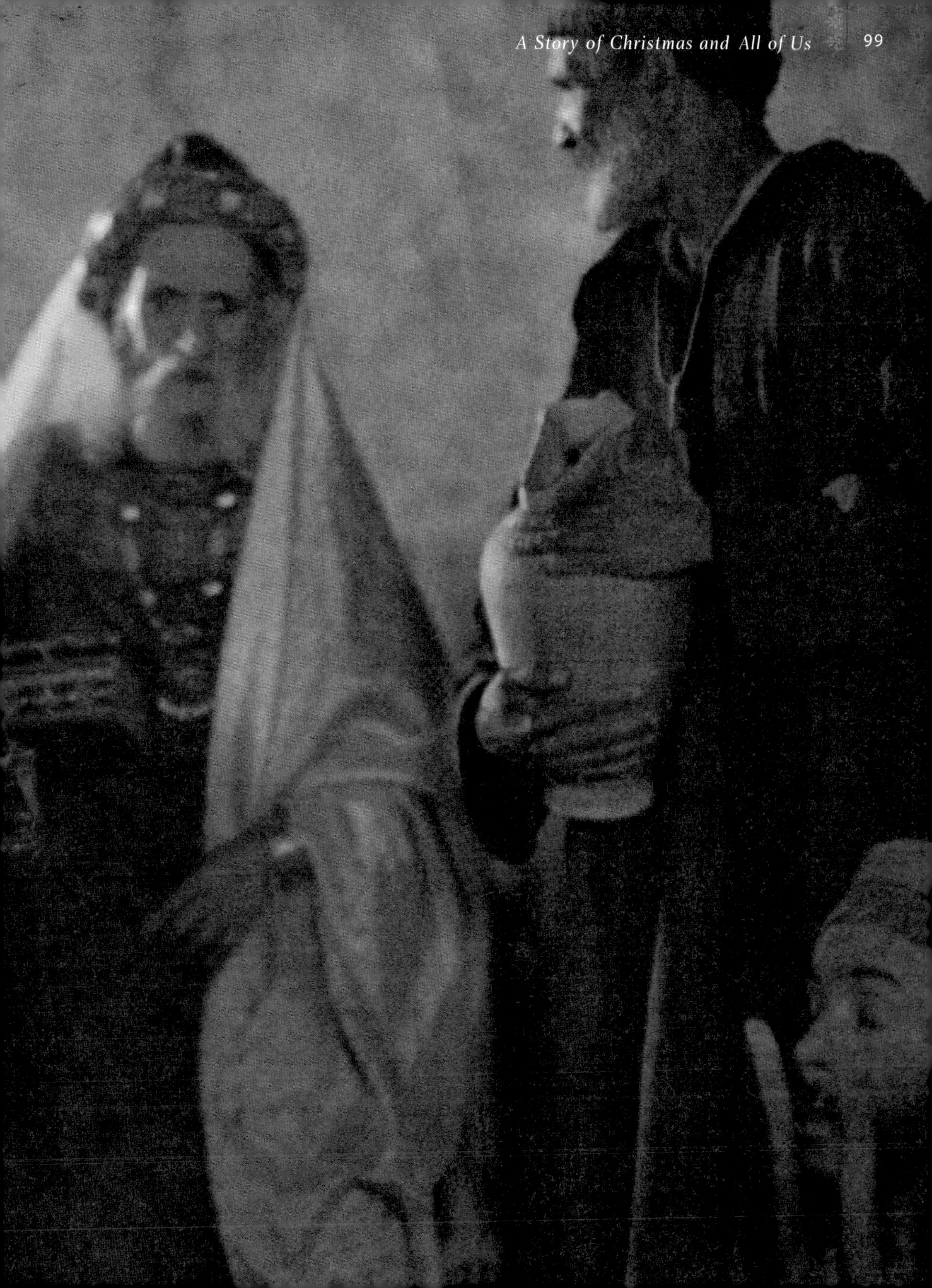

These fine kings all bow down on the dirty ground before the newborn Jesus and worship him.

It is well into the night before the crowd departs. The Magi do not return to tell Herod what they saw or where they found Jesus, because they learn in a dream that Herod has cruel intentions. They return to their homeland by a very different route.

Exhausted, Mary and Joseph are alone for the first time since Jesus' birth. The animals in their stalls are sound asleep, and the new parents soon fall into a deep slumber, too. The infant is swaddled and lying atop a feeding trough. The trough, which rests on a pile of hay, is called a manger.

Joseph lies on the floor next to Mary, his muscles aching from the long days on the road. It feels good to get some rest, and even better to know that their son has entered the world safely. In the morning they can be counted for the census. Soon they can return home to Nazareth, where Joseph's carpentry business awaits.

This routine of sleep and recovery in the grotto goes on for several days as Mary recovers her strength. Then one night, Joseph has a vivid dream, where he is running through the streets in the pouring rain. He hears a child screaming and Mary calling his name. He looks down and realizes that his feet are soaking wet. But they are not drenched in water; blood flows through the streets. That blood becomes a torrent, raging through the city like high tide. Joseph battles to stay on his feet. That screaming of a single child becomes the wail of hundreds. Joseph sees Herod's soldiers and the slashing of swords. He screams out for baby Jesus. He cannot be taken.

Joseph wakes up in a panic, hyperventilating. The dream felt

so real that he is actually stunned to behold Mary by the manger,

comforting the crying Jesus, the picture of serenity. But Joseph

knows better. He is a changed man since the angel appeared to

him. Joseph's belief in the words of the prophets has become

far deeper since he became a vital player in the fulfillment of

prophecy. He knows God speaks to prophets in many ways,

including dreams. Joseph is absolutely certain God has given

him the dream, and he knows what he must do next.

"We have to leave...."

Joseph doesn't have time to explain himself. "We have to leave immediately. I can't explain. Just trust me, Mary."

She pulls Jesus into her arms, holding him tightly, then nods to Joseph as he stands and gathers their belongings.

The same people who visited Jesus at his birth come to the aid of Mary and Joseph. Their departure from Bethlehem does not go unnoticed, and even in the dead of night, total strangers approach them and press parcels of food into their hands. These same strangers offer up prayers for them, making sure to get a last glimpse of this very special child before he disappears.

Soon Mary and Joseph reach the edge of town. Before them lies danger and uncertainty. They turn to look back at Bethlehem one last time. This small city will always have a special place in their hearts, even though they were there for just a few short days.

Turning again to look at the road in front of them, they see the torches atop the city walls of Jerusalem burning in the far distance. In another direction, to the east, the great star shines upon them like a compass beacon. Joseph pulls on the donkey's rope, choosing the eastward road. Within a few moments, Bethlehem isn't even visible in the distance, which is good—for Mary, Joseph, and their child, Jesus, have gotten out just in time.

With the dawn, Herod's soldiers ride into town. The captain of the guard, a man who never seems to grow tired of carrying out Herod's acts of barbarism, leads the charge. Teams of soldiers split up and scour the city streets.

Without a specific location for Jesus or even a description of his parents from the Magi, Herod has sent his army into Bethlehem to slaughter every male child under two years of age. He believes that is the only way to guarantee the murder of the right one.

Houses are broken into. Soldiers drag infants from their mothers' arms. The killing is beyond gruesome. Herod's soldiers kill without a second thought. No one counts how many innocents are slaughtered in Herod's purge, but the one child Herod wants has already escaped.

THE SUN RISES upon Joseph leading the donkey, with Mary holding the sleeping Jesus in her lap. Little do they understand the scene they have left behind.

Joseph undertakes an audacious plan to save Jesus: he will traverse a vast desert to take his family to Egypt. Joseph knows that it's a bold move, and he can only hope that the Pharaoh is kinder to his family than Herod. But the Romans also occupy Egypt, and a number of likeminded Jews have returned there, making for the second-largest Jewish community outside of Israel. He is retracing the footsteps of Moses in reverse: from the Promised Land, into the great wilderness where Moses wandered forty years, and then on into Egypt.

But someday Joseph wants to go home. He loves Nazareth, and he longs to raise his child there. But this young family cannot and will not return until Herod is either dead or no longer king—whichever comes first.

Jesus is free to grow up away from Herod's gaze. They make a home for themselves in Egypt and wait. Joseph prays that word will come soon when it is safe to go home. He doesn't have long to wait.

HEROD WILL NEVER KNOW that the slaughter of innocent children is for nothing. By the time Jesus reaches Egypt, Herod's life of debauchery has caught up with him. His face bloats and becomes covered with running sores; his joints become inflamed with gout and his liver fails, making it hard for him to eat or drink without discomfort; poor circulation has led to swelling and gangrene in his lower legs, making it almost impossible for him to walk.

Herod's mind is also failing, and his pathological need for control drives him on to one last disastrous act of brutality—the execution of his eldest son, Antipater, for plotting to overthrow him. With three younger sons of Herod looking on in horror, and despite Antipater's plea for mercy, Herod gestures to the executioner, who slips a noose around Antipater's throat and slowly strangles his son. Two soldiers drag Antipater's dead body out of the palace as Herod, breathing hard and groaning in pain, is helped to his throne.

When Herod dies, decades of resentment about Herod's treatment of priests, his subservience to Rome, his excessive taxation, and his brutality toward his subjects soon boils over. A collective rage engulfs Jerusalem. Statues of Herod are toppled, and images of his likeness are desecrated. Herod's kingdom is soon split between his three sons, who lack their father's brutal ability to control a nation. Anarchy ensues. Three thousand pilgrims, attempting to prevent the looting of a sacred temple, are murdered by authorities. Riots and revolts soon follow, which leads Rome to send in their own troops to restore order.

The Romans have a history of allowing people to embrace their own religions, but political dissent is the one thing they will not tolerate. The penalty for political dissent is crucifixion. A man is lashed to a tall pole, which features a horizontal crossbar. The arms are stretched wide on the crossbar and tied in place. His feet are nailed to the vertical pole. In some cases, spikes are driven through the hands to increase the pain of the punishment.

By the time Rome has quelled the disturbances brought on by

Herod's death, six thousand Jews have been sent into slavery and

more than two thousand have been crucified. Their bodies hang

in silhouette on hills surrounding the city as warning to those who

might also be considering dissent. The Romans' patience with

Herod's sons has worn quite thin, so they assume more and more

control of Jerusalem.

After Herod dies, an angel of the Lord appears in another dream to Joseph, telling him it is safe to end their exile. Jesus is a five-year-old boy as Mary and Joseph make their way back from Egypt. The long winding road takes them through the rocky hills toward Jerusalem.

"We're nearly there, Jesus," Mary says, holding Jesus on one of their two donkeys. "We're almost home."

As they come into a valley and head toward the north, Jesus is the first to turn his head and see the ghastly sight—the hill that towers over the valley road is lined with the bodies of the crucified.

"Joseph!" Mary cries out, looking on in disbelief. "Oh, God!

What have they done?" She is worried as never before. She looks

back toward Egypt, wondering if it would be better for them to

turn around and wait a few more years before returning home.

Joseph glances up on the rocky hill and sees the blackened

silhouetted shapes hanging on crosses. Immediately, he steps back

to Mary as she pulls young Jesus close and tries to cover his eyes

with her shawl. He takes her by the arm and says, "We must trust

in God's plan . . . as he trusts in us." He returns to the lead donkey,

determined to push on, staring grimly ahead the whole while.

When Joseph hears that Herod's son Archelaus, who inher-

ited his father's violent traits, is reigning in Judea, he is afraid to

go there. Having been warned in another dream, he withdraws

to the backwater region of Israel known as Galilee and takes the

family to live in the quiet city of Nazareth. So is fulfilled what

was said through the prophets: "He will be called a Nazarene,"

a righteous descendant of David whose wise and just rule will

bring God's salvation.

The one whom the angel proclaimed

as the promised King of the Jews,

the Messiah, has come home.

One day his words and deeds

will light a fire in the soul of Israel . . .

and change the world . . .

FOREVER.

Books and resources based on

THE BIBLE

EPIC MINISERIES

A Story of God and All of Us, "Novel"

A Story of God and All of Us, "100 Daily Reflections"

A Story of Christmas and All of Us

A Story of Easter and All of Us

THE BIBLE the Epic Miniseries, "Blu-ray and DVD"

THE BIBLE, "Music Inspired by the Epic Miniseries"

THE BIBLE, "The Official Soundtrack"

THE BIBLE, "30-Day Experience
for Churches and Small Groups"